Dear Parent:
Your child's love of reading

Every child learns to read in a different way and at his or her own speed. You can help your young reader improve and become more confident by encouraging his or her own interests and abilities. You can also guide your child's spiritual development by reading stories with biblical values and Bible stories, like I Can Read! books published by Zonderkidz. From books your child reads with you to the first books he or she reads alone, there are I Can Read! books for every stage of reading:

SHARED READING
Basic language, word repetition, and whimsical illustrations, ideal for sharing with your emergent reader.

BEGINNING READING
Short sentences, familiar words, and simple concepts for children eager to read on their own.

READING WITH HELP
Engaging stories, longer sentences, and language play for developing readers.

READING ALONE
Complex plots, challenging vocabulary, and high-interest topics for the independent reader.

ADVANCED READING
Short paragraphs, chapters, and exciting themes for the perfect bridge to chapter books.

I Can Read! books have introduced children to the joy of reading since 1957. Featuring award-winning authors and illustrators and a fabulous cast of beloved characters, I Can Read! books set the standard for beginning readers.

A lifetime of discovery begins with the magical words **"I Can Read!"**

Visit www.icanread.com for information on enriching your child's reading experience.
Visit www.zonderkidz.com for more Zonderkidz I Can Read! titles.

Whoever gathers money little by little makes it grow.
—*Proverbs 13:11*

ZONDERKIDZ

The Berenstain Bears® Piggy Bank Blessings
Copyright © 2013 by Berenstain Publishing, Inc.
Illustrations © 2013 by Berenstain Publishing, Inc.

Requests for information should be addressed to:
Zonderkidz, 5300 Patterson Ave SE, Grand Rapids, Michigan 49530

ISBN 978-0310-72505-3 (softcover)

Editor: Mary Hassinger
Design: Diane Mielke

Printed in China
13 14 15 16 17 18 /DSC/ 10 9 8 7 6 5 4 3 2 1

The Berenstain Bears
PIGGY BANK
BLESSINGS

Story and Pictures By

Stan & Jan Berenstain with Mike Berenstain

ZONDERVAN.com/
AUTHORTRACKER
follow your favorite authors

Brother and Sister Bear liked shopping

with Mama.

One day, Brother saw a toy he wanted.

Brother said, "May I have that toy plane?"

Mama said, "Yes."

Sister saw a teddy bear.

Sister said, "May I have that teddy?"

Mama said, "Yes."

But Mama did not say yes all the time.

"I want that truck too,"
Brother said.

Mama said, "No, not today."

"Why not?" asked Brother.

"You cannot have all the things
you want," said Mama.

"Why?" asked Sister.

Then Mama had an idea.

Mama bought a bank.

She said, "I will teach you

about money."

The new bank looked like a small pig.

It had a slot for money.

"The Bible says we should all

set aside some money.

This will help you save,"

Mama said.

Mama told the cubs about
saving money for something special.
She told them when they got money
as gifts it should go in the bank.

Sometimes
they got pennies.

Sometimes
they got nickels …

or dimes …

or quarters.

And sometimes
they got dollar bills!

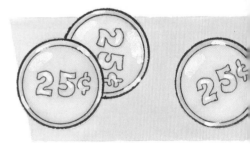

Brother and Sister got money

for the jobs they did.

They emptied trash.

They watered flowers.

They pulled weeds.

Mama had told them
they should save for
something special.
And that is just what
the cubs did.

One day Mama said, "You cubs
are doing a good job saving."
"Thank you," said Sister.
"But when we want to use it for
something special, how will we
get the money out?"
Mama said, "You will know
when the time comes."

Then one day, Brother and Sister
knew the time had come.
They needed the money for
something special.
Sister said, "Now how do we
get the money out?"

"There's only one way
to do it," Brother said.

He got his toy hammer.

CRASH went the piggy bank.

The money spilled out.

Brother and Sister took their money.

They ran out of the tree house.

Later, Mama saw the broken bank.

"Oh dear," said Mama.

"As Proverbs says, 'Cast but a glance at riches

and they are gone, for they will surely

sprout wings and fly off …'" she said.

"I hope they are using their

money wisely.

Just then, the door opened.

In came Brother and Sister.

They each had a huge lollipop.

"Cubs!" Mama said.

"You were saving for something special."

Mama did not see the small

box the cubs were hiding.

"We did, Mama," Sister said.

Mama said, "Lollipops are not special!"
She did not think Brother and Sister
had learned all about saving.

"We know," said Brother.
"But YOU are special, Mama,"
said Sister.
"Here is your birthday gift."

Mama said, "Oh dear!

It IS my birthday tomorrow.

May I open it now?"

"Yes!" said the cubs.

Mama's gift was a watch.

She was thankful to God

for her two loving cubs.

"What a fine gift," said Mama.

"Thank you.

But where did you get the lollipops?"

Brother said, "We got your watch
at Mr. Jones' store.
He gave them to us for being
such nice cubs."

"Mr. Jones is right about that.
You are nice cubs," said Mama.
"And like the Good Book says,
'their children will be a blessing.'"

And Mama gave Brother and Sister
a big bear hug.